JOB DISCOVERY

JOBS IF YOU LIKE SPORTS

by Roxanne Troup

BrightPoint Press

San Diego, CA

BrightPoint Press

an imprint of ReferencePoint Press, Inc.
Printed in the United States

For more information, contact:
BrightPoint Press
PO Box 27779
San Diego, CA 92198
www.BrightPointPress.com

LIBRARY OF CONGRESS CATALOGING-IN-PUBLICATION DATA

Names: Troup, Roxanne, author.
Title: Jobs if you like sports / by Roxanne Troup.
Description: San Diego, CA: BrightPoint, [2025] | Series: Job discovery | Includes bibliographical references and index. | Audience: Grades 7-9
Identifiers: LCCN 2024001074 (print) | LCCN 2024001075 (eBook) | ISBN 9781678209209 (hardcover) | ISBN 9781678209216 (eBook)
Subjects: LCSH: Sports--Vocational guidance--Juvenile literature. | Vocational guidance--Juvenile literature.
Classification: LCC GV734.3 .T76 2025 (print) | LCC GV734.3 (eBook) | DDC 796.023--dc23/eng/20240111
LC record available at https://lccn.loc.gov/2024001074
LC eBook record available at https://lccn.loc.gov/2024001075

CONTENTS

THE SPORTS INDUSTRY AT A GLANCE 4

INTRODUCTION 6
SECOND CHANCES

CHAPTER ONE 10
SPORTSCASTER

CHAPTER TWO 22
ATHLETIC DIRECTOR

CHAPTER THREE 34
EXERCISE PHYSIOLOGIST

CHAPTER FOUR 46
SPORTS PUBLIC RELATIONS

Other Jobs in the Sports Industry 58
Glossary 60
Source Notes 61
Index 62
Image Credits 63
About the Author 64

THE SPORTS INDUSTRY AT A GLANCE

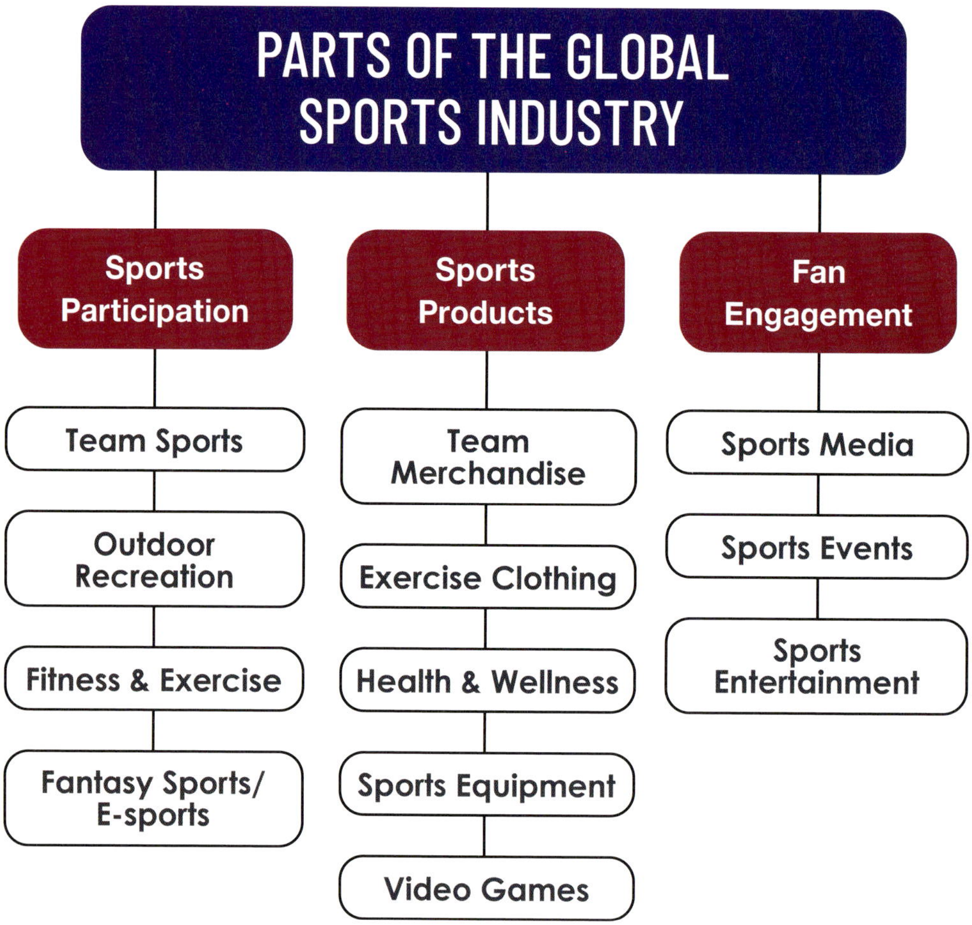

Source: Roger Best and Dennis Howard. "The Business of Sports." Global Sports Insights, *2023. www.globalsportsinsights.com.*

NUMBER OF HIGH SCHOOL, COLLEGE, AND PRO ATHLETES IN MOST POPULAR SPORTS

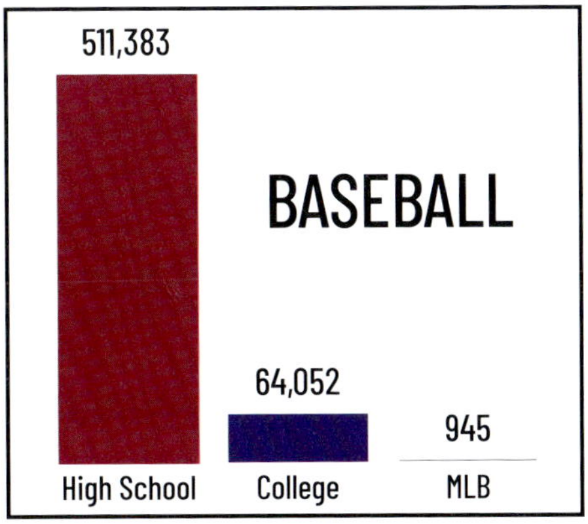

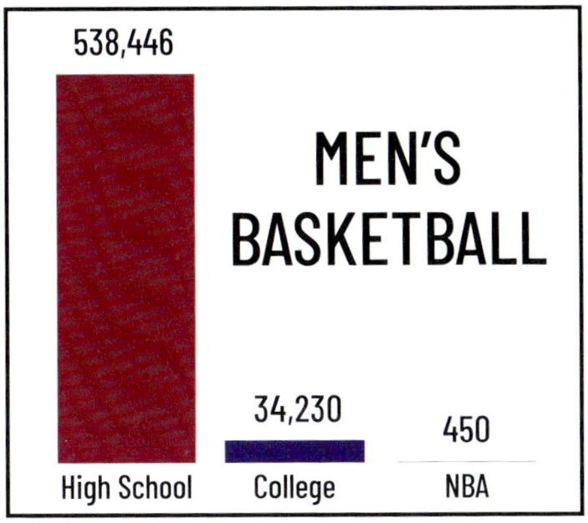

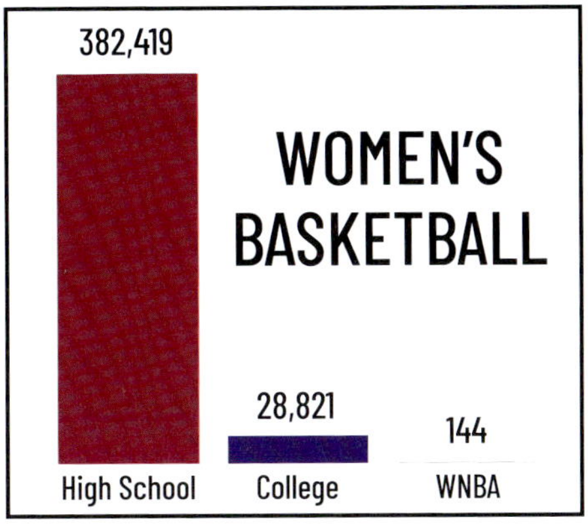

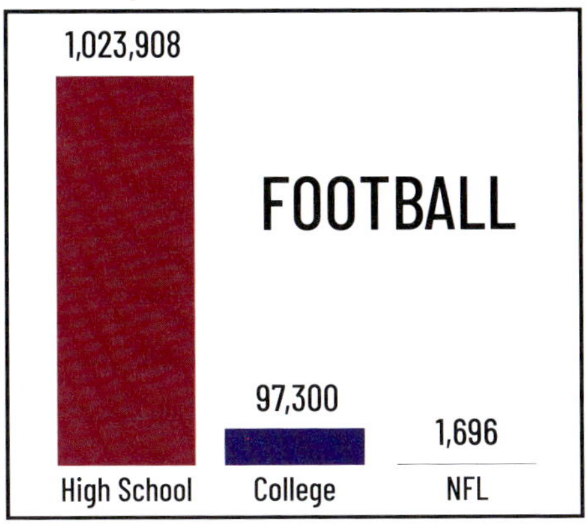

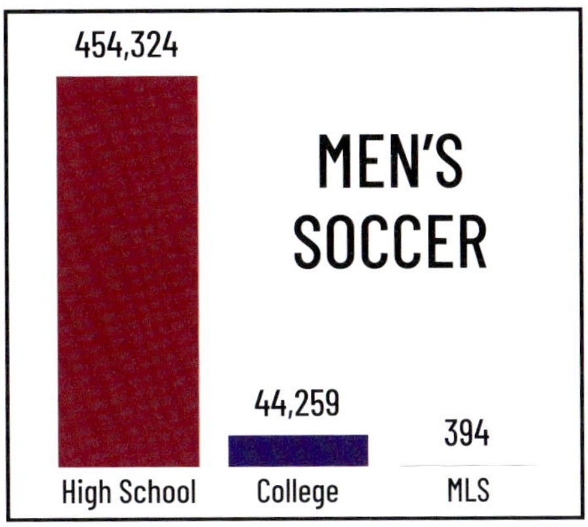

Source: Patrick O'Rourke. "Play Your Sport in College!" Scholarship Stats.com, *2020. www.scholarshipstats.com.*

SECOND CHANCES

James Brown was built for sports. JB ran drills. He practiced shooting. He spent his free time on the court. JB's hard work paid off. He became an All-American athlete. JB was recruited to play college basketball. Then, he was drafted by the Atlanta Hawks. It looked like his dream of playing in the NBA would come true.

Brown hoped to have a career with the NBA. But he did not work as hard

After his pro basketball days, James Brown began a career as a sportscaster.

as he had in high school. JB was cut from the team. He did not want to waste another opportunity.

In 1978, JB began covering basketball games for a local television network. He carefully prepared for each game. Soon he became a sports anchor. This time, he worked hard to improve. JB took speech classes. Slowly he worked his way up. He became a network host. In 2020, he was inducted into the Sports Broadcasting Hall of Fame.

WHAT IS THE SPORTS INDUSTRY?

Most players never become professional athletes. But a person who loves sports can still work in the field. Like JB, they may become a sportscaster. They could coach.

There are many jobs in the sports field for those who want to stay close to the action.

Or they could become an athletic director. They might work in sports medicine. Or they could join a public relations team.

The sports industry is huge. There are people who work to organize and promote sporting events. Other jobs involve fitness products. People may sell or market clothing, sports equipment, and energy bars.

CHAPTER ONE

SPORTSCASTER

Sportscasters are a type of reporter. They are also called announcers. Sportscasters cover live games or events. They help fans follow along. Sportscasters work with camera operators and audio engineers. They also work with television producers.

Graham McNamee was one of the first sportscasters. He called World Series games in the 1920s and 1930s.

Sportscasters deliver reports at professional and amateur sporting events.

ESPN

McNamee helped radio listeners picture the game in their minds. Curt Smith is a broadcast historian. He explained what people liked about McNamee. "[McNamee] understood the listener would remain with

Sportscaster

Education: 4-year degree in communications or journalism

Personal Qualities: Knowledgeable about sports, a good communicator, confident, well-spoken, intuitive, well-connected

Working Conditions: Sportscasters work long hours both in front of and behind the camera. Their on-air work is fast-paced and collaborative. Behind the scenes, they do a lot of research. Sportscasters often work weekends and evenings. They travel often.

Average Salary: $70,270

Former competitive athletes sometimes turn to sportscasting as their next career.

you as long as you entertained," Smith said. "His first commandment was, 'I will not bore you,' and he never did."[1]

Sportscasters do more than explain the game. There are two broadcasters in the booth. The play-by-play person describes the game's action. The other is usually a former athlete or coach who knows the game well. This person is the analyst. They comment on strategies and plays.

They may talk about their own playing or coaching days.

Swimmer Michael Phelps is the most decorated Olympic athlete of all time. He later became a sportscaster. Molly Solomon is a producer. She explained what she liked about his first broadcast. "From the moment he joined our team at Trials, Michael's ability to provide insightful analysis [and] thoughtful commentary and tell entertaining stories was apparent," she said.[2]

TRAINING AND SKILLS

Like Phelps, some sportscasters are retired athletes. Others are sports fans. Most study communications or journalism in college. The classes help students learn to speak in public. They teach good interviewing skills.

A pleasant voice and friendly personality are important for a sportscaster. Students can take other classes to learn technical skills. Script writing, photography, and video editing are common. These skills provide more job options after graduation.

Syracuse University is known for sportscasting. So is Northwestern University. These schools encourage

No Average Joe

Not all top broadcasters went to top broadcasting schools. Joe Davis went to tiny Beloit College in Wisconsin. He called sporting events at the school. After college, he announced minor league baseball games. In 2017, he was hired by the Los Angeles Dodgers. Davis did the national television broadcast of the World Series in 2022.

students to stay connected after graduation. Sometimes graduates mentor current students. University of Missouri, University of Southern California, and Arizona State also have good programs. Each of these schools focuses on hands-on learning. Students produce school news broadcasts. They announce athletic games.

Most schools connect students with internships. Some universities offer advanced degrees. These things can help a student stand out.

HOW TO GET STARTED

An internship is an important first step. This is a temporary job. It may be paid or unpaid. Recruiter Carolyne Savini says it's hard to get a job if the applicant doesn't

Television internships might involve working inside a production studio.

have internship experience. Local radio and TV stations offer internships. Sports teams do as well.

Joining the National Sports Media Association (NSMA) is a good way to meet people in the field. NSMA offers internships. It also accepts student content for its website. The organization helps students connect with professionals. They provide feedback on student work. Some colleges have NSMA chapters on campus.

The Sports Industry Networking and Career (SINC) Conference is another way for students to make connections. Students can meet young professionals and industry leaders. They learn about industry trends.

Those who want to work for major networks need a talent agent. These people manage careers. They help clients meet people. And they point out areas where clients can improve.

FUTURE DIRECTIONS

More people watch news and sports online. This has made media companies think about how to gain **market share**. Big companies may buy streaming services.

Broadcast networks may buy other networks. This allows more people to watch their content. That content is presented in

With so many games being broadcast online, the need for sportscasters is greater than ever.

many ways for different audiences. This provides more chances for sportscasters.

The internet has also changed the way sportscasters can get noticed. They can post audition tapes online for employers to see. Many young broadcasters start their own podcasts. Others create sports content for YouTube. Gaining followers online can often lead to bigger opportunities.

FIND OUT MORE

American Sportscasters Association
www.americansportscastersonline.com
The American Sportscasters Association promotes quality sportscasting. It offers various awards programs to recognize sportscasters who excel in the field.

National Sports Media Association
www.nationalsportsmedia.org
The National Sports Media Association serves those who want to work in sports media. It offers mentorship and networking opportunities. It also provides internships and scholarships.

CHAPTER TWO

ATHLETIC DIRECTOR

Athletic directors lead athletic programs. They are often called ADs. ADs work in schools or colleges. Community programs like the YMCA also have athletic directors. ADs hire coaches. They create game schedules and organize sporting events. ADs also raise funds and manage budgets.

ADs at colleges and schools work with agencies that oversee sports.

Athletic directors may run sports complexes that have indoor and outdoor facilities.

These agencies organize schools into leagues. They adopt rules for sports games. Agencies also set rules for athletes to follow. Some rules limit how often an athlete can compete. Others restrict

Athletic Director

Education: 4-year degree in education or sports management

Personal Qualities: An experienced coach, a good leader, well-organized, analytical, positive

Certification and Licensing: Varies by state

Working Conditions: ADs work in an office environment during school hours. They often work weekends and evening hours to support games.

Average Salary: $71,311

Coaches at schools and community centers report to athletic directors.

off-season practices. It's an AD's job to make sure their school follows these rules.

TRAINING AND SKILLS

Most athletic directors have a 4-year degree. Many study physical education. Others study sport administration or business. These degrees help ADs develop communication and organizational skills. At higher levels, ADs typically hold master's degrees.

ADs have many tasks. Good business and marketing skills are important. ADs also need management skills. They hire and oversee coaches and referees.

Many ADs were once athletes and coaches. They understand the importance of good leadership. ADs **mediate** disputes.

Equal Opportunity

In 1972, the US government passed Title IX regulations. Title IX gave women equal access to education. No one could be excluded from public school programs based on their gender. In 1975, the law expanded to include athletics. ADs make sure Title IX is upheld.

They face losing seasons. But they remember the words of head coach Vince Lombardi. He said, "The achievements of an organization are the results of the combined effort of each individual."[3]

ADs who work in schools are often teachers or administrators. They must pass a background check. Some ADs also need basic medical training. They learn to prevent and identify **concussions**. They are trained in CPR. They learn to use a **defibrillator**. This allows ADs to provide emergency care until an ambulance arrives.

HOW TO GET STARTED

Most athletic directors are coaches first. Kevin Garner is a coach and AD from Missouri. Garner studied physical education in college. After graduation, Garner was hired to coach at a small school. He gained experience and moved to larger schools. As a coach, he won many awards. Eventually, he became an AD in Rolla, Missouri. Garner was interviewed by the *Quincy Herald-Whig*. He said his coaching experience helped him as an AD. He knew the challenges coaches face. That made him a better communicator.

Like Garner, candidates with experience often get the best jobs. Students can volunteer with community organizations like the YMCA to gain experience. The Y trains volunteer coaches and referees to run its youth sports programs.

Students also apply for internships. Interning provides references for a first job.

Volunteering to coach youth sports teams provides good experience for future ADs.

These are recommendations from people who know the candidate well. Employers check references to confirm the skills and work habits of a candidate.

Connecting with others in the sports industry is important. According to the editors at *Jobs in Sports*, knowing the person who is hiring for the job can make all the difference. Attending AD conferences is a good way to meet people. The National Interscholastic Athletic Administrators Association (NIAAA) offers one each year.

FUTURE DIRECTIONS

Most athletic directors are male. But that is changing. In 2019, nearly 24 percent of college-level ADs were women. In some regions, that number was higher. In the

Mid-Eastern Athletic Conference (MEAC), five of the eight ADs are women. The National Collegiate Athletic Association (NCAA) is committed to gender equality. That number is likely to rise.

A big part of an athletic director's job is working with technologies that schools use to track statistics and broadcast games.

As technologies develop, the work of ADs is changing. Scheduling and team communications tasks are now done online. Families are also requesting that games be livestreamed. Taking video of events may sometimes be an AD's job. Virtual platforms such as Hudl can be used for streaming games. Software like SportsConnect can help track stats and ticket sales. This software can also help ADs monitor team social media accounts. These new technologies make an AD's job a little easier.

FIND OUT MORE

National High School Coaches Association

www.nhsca.com

This nonprofit organization supports coaches by providing continuing education opportunities. It also shares updated safety resources and celebrates excellent programs.

National Interscholastic Athletic Administrators Association

www.members.niaaa.org

The National Interscholastic Athletic Administrators Association offers leadership development for ADs and coaches. It also organizes a conference each year. Members can network with others and hear about issues affecting the industry.

Sports Management Degrees

www.sports-management-degrees.com

Sports Management Degrees website is an online degree guide for students. It gives an overview of the sports management industry and provides information about colleges.

CHAPTER THREE

EXERCISE PHYSIOLOGIST

Exercise physiologists (EPs) work in sports medicine. They treat or work to prevent injuries. EPs also help improve how athletes perform. An EP plans fitness programs for athletes. Some work as coaches or trainers. Others work in hospitals and rehab centers. EPs might monitor heart issues while patients exercise. They help patients with **chronic** conditions.

Exercise physiologists help athletes stretch and perform exercises properly.

Some EPs even help companies develop exercise equipment.

Working with an EP can make a big difference for athletes. Football player Trace Armstrong says, "The greatest investment you can make is in your body."[4] Caring for

Exercise Physiologist

Education: 4-year degree in exercise science

Personal Qualities: Athletic, compassionate, detail-oriented, social, accommodating, analytical

Certification and Licensing: CPR and basic medical certification required; licensing varies by state

Working Conditions: EPs mostly work indoors during office hours. Many EPs work in gyms, rehab centers, and doctors' offices.

Average Salary: $51,350

their body can extend an athlete's career. In 2010, Indianapolis Colts quarterback Peyton Manning pinched a nerve in his neck. It affected his ability to throw a football. He had many surgeries to correct it. No one knew if he would heal. So, the Colts cut him.

After the surgeries, Manning's arm felt weak. The pain was gone. But he struggled to throw. Manning began working with his old college coach. Coach David Cutcliffe was not an EP. But he guided Manning through his recovery. He used an EP approach. Cutcliffe did not want to stress Manning's body. He created a program to help Manning. It focused on rebuilding his strength. Cutcliffe talked about his approach in a 2020 interview. "We have the science . . . we measure every practice," Cutcliffe said. "We have heart rate monitors, player load monitors. I'm going to study it. I'm going to see how far we can physically move that needle without . . . injuries."[5]

Cutcliffe helped Manning improve his grip strength. He showed Manning how to change his arm motion. Gradually, Manning relearned to throw a ball. Soon he was throwing better than ever. In 2012, Manning signed with the Denver Broncos. He played

Exercise Is Healthy

Dr. Gustav Zander was an early EP. He developed the first mechanical exercise equipment in the late 1800s. Zander's machines used weights, levers, and pulleys to adjust resistance. Many of his machine designs are still used today.

EPs sometimes take athletes' blood pressure before exercise to measure the effect of exertion on the heart.

four more seasons before retiring. He led his new team to the Super Bowl twice.

TRAINING AND SKILLS

Education programs for EPs vary. Most EPs need a 4-year degree. Degrees in exercise science or health are best. These degrees include clinicals in hospitals or clinics. Students learn from doctors and other EPs. They work directly with patients.

EPs study the patient's medical history. They often run stress and fitness tests for clients. They also monitor **vital signs**. Students learn how to do this in their classes. They also study anatomy and body movement. These classes help EP students develop exercise programs for their clients. Most states require EPs to be trained in basic life support measures as well.

Sports medicine organizations provide industry certifications. Examples include the American Society of Exercise Physiologists and the American College of Sports Medicine. To be certified, members must finish college and pass a test. Members must take more courses every 3 to 5 years to stay certified. As of 2023, only Louisiana requires an EP to be licensed.

HOW TO GET STARTED

The EP profession doesn't have set rules about education. This makes it hard for EPs to prove their skills. Most employers hire people based on their experience. EPs can gain experience through clinicals and internships. Some college programs require

Working as a personal trainer can be a good way to gain experience for a career in exercise physiology.

students to complete clinicals to graduate. Students can intern at area hospitals or clinics. They can also look for internships on the Clinical Exercise Physiology Association website.

To work in the sports field, candidates usually need an entry-level job. Positions in fitness centers and hospitals rarely use the term *exercise physiologist*. Instead, these people are often called *wellness coaches* or *personal trainers*. These positions can be a good way to launch a career as an EP.

A strong resume can help land a job in exercise physiology. Applicants should include internships on their resumes. They should also note any certifications they've earned. And they should provide details about any clinical experience.

Studies show that exercise can be as beneficial for mental health as it is for physical health.

FUTURE DIRECTIONS

An idea called exercise is medicine (EIM) has led to more jobs for EPs. EIM includes physical activity as part of a patient's care. Annabel at Longevity PT says, "If exercise could be packaged in a pill, it would be the single most widely prescribed and beneficial medicine."[6]

Others agree. *Medical News Today* says that exercise can be used to treat anxiety and depression. And Harvard Health says that regular exercise can slow the signs of aging.

Education and certification programs will need to be improved for this field to grow. Currently, there is not a set program used to educate or certify EPs. The American Society of Exercise Physiologists is working to change that.

FIND OUT MORE

American College of Sports Medicine
www.acsm.org

The American College of Sports Medicine provides resources, education, and career certification for sports medicine students. Members have mentorship opportunities and can apply for research grants. They also receive discounts on conferences.

American Society of Exercise Physiologists
www.asep.org

The American Society of Exercise Physiologists is a union of exercise physiologists. It provides program accreditation. The organization publishes several industry journals. It also holds many conferences and workshops for people in the field.

SPORTS PUBLIC RELATIONS

Public relations (PR) is a type of marketing. PR creates and manages the public images of organizations, people, and brands. In sports, PR people are hired to manage teams or players. They promote client brands using social media. They also use **press releases** and interviews. And, when there's a problem, the PR person figures out how to communicate about it.

Public relations teams work together to come up with marketing plans.

They explain bad news in a way that won't hurt the player as much.

PR works closely with marketing directors and social media managers. They make sure brand images and messages are consistent. PR professionals also work with sponsors. Sponsorships and endorsements

Sports Public Relations

Education: 4-year degree in marketing or communications

Personal Qualities: Honest, reliable, a good communicator, organized, a good problem solver, influential, creative

Working Conditions: PR professionals mainly work in an office setting.

Average Salary: $67,440

help their clients make money. This is when a brand pays an athlete to use their product.

Some PR professionals work on commission. This means they earn a portion of their client's pay. More endorsements equal more money. Other PR professionals earn a fee for every project they complete for their clients. Doing a good job for one client helps them find more clients.

Ronda Rousey is a mixed martial arts fighter. She is endorsed by companies like Monster Energy and Reebok. These deals have earned her over $5 million. Each endorsement increases the number of people who recognize her. A bigger audience makes Rousey more valuable to companies and fight coordinators. She can use that to ask for a higher salary.

PR guru Ronn Torossian explains how athletes use PR. He says, "Athletes will continue to have influence even after their peak athleticism fades, so long as they play the PR game just as well as their sport of choice."[7]

A Long Shot

In 1984, Nike hired a star college athlete to wear their shoes. No one knew then how famous Michael Jordan would become. But he changed the sponsorship model. In addition to earning a one-time fee for "Air Jordans," he asked for **royalties**. He has been retired for more than 20 years. But Jordan continues to earn royalties off this deal.

TRAINING AND SKILLS

There are many paths to a career in PR. Some focus on digital media. Others serve a specific type of client. They may only work with basketball players. Or they might specialize in women's athletics. But all PR agents learn one important thing. Their audience's love of sport can be used to benefit their clients.

Most people in PR study public relations, marketing, or social sciences. Communications and business degrees are also helpful. Social science classes teach problem-solving skills. Good PR agents are organized. They know how to do many things at once. PR people adapt to new situations quickly. And they know how to form good relationships with the media.

Communication skills and the ability to work with a team are important for a public relations career.

HOW TO GET STARTED

The right college programs can help students gain PR experience while still in school. Most colleges offer entry-level jobs to students. Working in campus activity offices or with student organizations can provide opportunities to use PR skills. Jobs that develop organization and public speaking skills can also be helpful.

Colleges often connect students with internship opportunities. An internship with a media or marketing company is especially helpful. Newspaper and radio stations offer internships. Marketing interns develop research and teamwork skills. They learn to identify a target audience. Media interns perfect their writing and pitching skills. A pitch is an email or letter to a potential client. It describes a marketing idea.

Each of these opportunities helps students build their portfolios. Portfolios include examples of a person's work. PR portfolios feature sample press releases and media pitches. They highlight social media **case studies**. Portfolios can also include sample art designs.

Students should also follow what is happening in the industry. They can join organizations like the Public Relations Society of America (PRSA). Or they could attend conferences with the National Sports Forum.

FUTURE DIRECTIONS

Use of social media is growing quickly. In April 2023, there were 4.8 billion social media users. Those users spent an average of 2.5 hours a day on social media.

Social media has become the modern press conference. When all eyes are on a team, player, or sports company, it is important to be on brand.

Sports teams, businesses, and organizations want to build their social media presence. They hope to create stronger relationships with customers. Companies also want to stand out from their competitors. This means more companies are hiring PR personnel to manage their image.

FIND OUT MORE

National Sport Marketing Network
https://sportsmarketingnetwork.com
The National Sport Marketing Network is a professional organization for sports marketers. It provides career services. These include help with resumes and job searches. It also offers networking opportunities.

Public Relations Society of America
www.prsa.org
The Public Relations Society of America is a professional development and networking association. It promotes diversity and ethics within the industry. It also offers accreditation to its members.

Sport Marketing Association
www.sportmarketingassociation.com
The Sport Marketing Association provides information about sport marketing. It also holds an annual conference where students and industry professionals can network.

OTHER JOBS IN THE SPORTS INDUSTRY

Sports Data Analyst

A sports analyst collects player and team data. They also gather game statistics. Analysts look for patterns in the data. They make connections and interpret the meaning of those connections. They try to predict future performance. Analysts also track statistics that fans use to learn more about their favorite players.

Biomechanical Engineer

Biomechanics is the study of human motion. In sports, it explains the connection between athletes and their equipment. These engineers teach athletes the correct way to move for their sport. Athletes use these tips to improve performance and prevent injuries. Biomechanical engineers also help develop prosthetics and better sports equipment. They create software to help athletes map their movements.

Event Planner

Event planners organize sporting events. They plan every detail so athletes, coaches, fans, and officials have a good experience. Planners reserve facilities. They make sure the facilities are clean and staffed. They invite teams to compete and arrange their travel and lodging. Planners also work with media teams to promote and record the event.

Groundskeeper

Groundskeepers care for the different surfaces of a baseball field, football field, or soccer pitch. They inspect the grass or sand to see if these areas need any repair. Groundskeepers also maintain grass by reseeding worn patches. They water and mow the turf as needed. Baseball groundskeepers also care for the infield sand. They make sure it is flattened and even before games. Some groundskeepers may work at a stadium. Others maintain community recreational fields.

GLOSSARY

case studies

intensive studies of specific people or events

chronic

long lasting

concussions

brain injuries caused by head trauma

defibrillator

a machine that uses electricity to restore a heartbeat to the correct rhythm

market share

a part of an industry or market controlled by a company

mediate

to work with people who disagree to reach an agreement

press releases

official statements about events or people

royalties

money paid to someone for the right to use their image, name, words, art, or other asset

vital signs

measurements that show how well a person's body is working

SOURCE NOTES

CHAPTER ONE: SPORTSCASTER

1. Quoted in "Graham McNamee," *National Baseball Hall of Fame*, n.d. www.baseballhall.org.

2. Quoted in Jackie Strause, "Michael Phelps Joins NBC's Olympics Broadcast Team," *The Hollywood Reporter*, July 19, 2021. www.hollywoodreporter.com.

CHAPTER TWO: ATHLETIC DIRECTOR

3. Quoted in Dr. Richard Carter, "Leaders Are Made Not Born: Vince Lombardi," *Switch*, September 29, 2017. www.switcheducation.com.

CHAPTER THREE: EXERCISE PHYSIOLOGIST

4. Quoted in Peter King, "Stretching the Field," *Sport's Illustrated Vault*, November 5, 2012. www.vault.si.com.

5. Quoted in Shawn Krest, "David Cutcliffe on Duke's Conditioning: We Have to Go to Plan B," *Sports Illustrated*, October 1, 2020. www.si.com.

6. Quoted in "Exercise Physiology—A Growing Profession!" *Longevity*, February 19, 2023. www.longevitypt.com.

CHAPTER FOUR: SPORTS PUBLIC RELATIONS

7. Quoted in Ronn Torossian, "Public Relations and the World's Leading Athletes," *Forbes*, January 12, 2017. www.forbes.com.

INDEX

Armstrong, Trace, 36
athletic directors, 9, 22–33

Brown, James, 6–8
business degrees, 25, 51

certifications, 24, 36, 40, 42, 44, 45
coaches, 13, 22, 24, 26–28, 33, 34, 37, 42
communications, 12, 14, 26, 32, 48, 51
Cutcliffe, David, 37–38

Davis, Joe, 15

exercise physiologists, 34–45
exercise science, 36, 39

Garner, Kevin, 27–28
gender equality, 26, 31

internships, 16–17, 21, 28, 41-42, 53

Jordan, Michael, 50
journalism, 12, 14

Lombardi, Vince, 27

Manning, Peyton, 37–39
marketing, 46, 48, 51, 53, 57
McNamee, Graham, 10, 13

National Sports Forum, 54
National Sports Media Association, 17, 21

personal training, 42
Phelps, Michael, 14
physical education degrees, 25, 27
portfolios, 53–54
public relations, 9, 46–57

Rousey, Ronda, 49–50

social media, 32, 46, 48, 54–56
Solomon, Molly, 14
sport administration, 25
Sports Broadcasting Hall of Fame, 8
sports management degrees, 24, 33
sports medicine, 9, 34, 40, 45
sportscasters, 8, 10–21

Title IX, 26
Torossian, Ronn, 50
trainers, 34

wellness coaches, 42

YMCA, 22, 28

Zander, Dr. Gustav, 38

IMAGE CREDITS

Cover: © wavebreakmedia/Shutterstock Images
4: © Red Line Editorial
5: © Red Line Editorial
7: © Debby Wong/Shutterstock Images
9: © Stephen Reeves/Shutterstock Images
11: © Maxisport/Shutterstock Images
13: © A.PAES/Shutterstock Images
17: © Borhax/Shutterstock Images
19: © Eduard Goricev/Shutterstock Images
23: © sandsun/Shutterstock Images
25: © Rawpixel.com/Shutterstock Images
29: © tammykayphoto/Shutterstock Images
31: © Eyecrave Productions/iStockphoto
35: © dusanpetkovic/iStockphoto
39: © Andriiii/Shutterstock Images
41: © stockfour/Shutterstock Images
43: © PeopleImages/iStockphoto
47: © andresr/iStockphoto
52: © fizkes/iStockphoto
55: © microgen/iStockphoto
58 (top): © Ground Picture/Shutterstock Images
58 (bottom): © Jacob Lund/Shutterstock Images
59 (top): © SolStock/iStockphoto
59 (bottom): © Conor P. Fitzgerald/Shutterstock Images

ABOUT THE AUTHOR

With a background in education, Roxanne Troup writes children's books that entertain, educate, and inspire. She lives in the mountains of Colorado with her family and enjoys visiting schools to promote literacy.